WAY PAST MAD

Hallee Adelman

illustrated by Sandra de la Prada

Albert Whitman & Company
Chicago, Illinois

To Sivonn, Grant, Hudson, and anyone who gets mad—HA

To Miquel and Jordi—SP

Library of Congress Cataloging-in-Publication data is on file with the publisher.

Text copyright © 2020 by Hallee Adelman
Illustrations copyright © 2020 by Albert Whitman & Company
Illustrations by Sandra de la Prada
First published in the United States of America in 2020
by Albert Whitman & Company
ISBN 978-0-8075-8685-3 (hardcover)
ISBN 978-0-8075-8683-9 (ebook)

Printed in China
10 9 8 7 6 5 4 3 2 WKT 24 23 22 21 20

Design by Nina Simoneaux

For more information about Albert Whitman & Company,
visit our website at www.albertwhitman.com.

Nate messed up my room. It made me mad.

Then he fed Axe my breakfast.
So I ate toast.
I hate toast.

He even ruined my favorite hat.
I loved that hat.
Mom said, "Nate's little, Keya. He didn't mean it."
Now I felt really mad.

I flung open the screen door and called, "Bye."
But my family was too busy to hear me.

I headed to school, kicking rocks and sticks as I walked.
Kicking and kicking and kicking.
I was way past mad.
The kind of mad
that starts
and swells
and spreads like a rash.

I stopped to fold down
the top of my sock
to cover the hole where my skin peeked through.
That Nate! He must've cut that hole.

"Wait up!" my friend Hooper called.

But this morning, I wasn't gonna wait for anyone. I ran.
"Wait up, Keya!"

I looked back at Hooper and ran even faster...
Like I was the best runner in the world.
Racing,
leaving all others in the dust,
far behind me...

The crowd roaring,
calling my name
so loud
as I cross that line...
without Nate messing anything up.

Then I'd stand tall,
wearing brand new socks
and a gold medal like sunshine around my neck.

I ran and ran, but the sidewalk was crooked.
KER-THUNK!
Stupid sidewalk.

"You okay, Keya?" Hooper asked.
"Do I look okay?" I sassed, pointing to my knee.
But Hooper wasn't looking at my knee.
He was looking at
that hole
in my sock.
The hole that felt
everywhere.

I stood up fast.
"Leave me alone!"
"What? Why?"
"Because I don't like you, Hooper."
Which wasn't even true. But my mad made me say it.
My heart sank. I knew I hurt Hooper's feelings.

I watched Hooper head toward school,
kicking rocks and sticks as he walked.
Kicking and kicking and kicking, like he was way past mad.

He was too far away when I whispered,
"I didn't mean to give you my mad, Hooper."

But like he actually heard me, Hooper stopped for a second.
I don't know why.
I just know that I was glad he did.
So I called, "Hooper! Hooper! Wait up!"
But he didn't wait.

I called again, "Please, Hooper, wait up!"
He looked back at me.
But then he kept on going.
Running up our favorite slide,
calling out to Skitter and Jin.

And I didn't want to be way past mad anymore. I wanted to be with Hooper.

I ran toward him like
the best runner in the world,
and I didn't care
which way my socks flipped or if Nate
was messing things up at home.
I just cared about reaching Hooper
and saying,

"I'm sorry. I like you a lot."

After I said it, I felt better.
And Hooper didn't look mad.
He said, "I know. Come on."

I told him about my morning.
And how Mom said Nate didn't mean it.
And how I didn't mean it when I hurt
Hooper's feelings.
Then we joked and laughed.

I was so happy.
The kind of happy
that starts
and swells
and spreads like a smile.

We turned the corner, and headed the right way...

Together.